Trouble at the Treasury

CAPITAL MYSTERIES 7

by Ron Roy
illustrated by Timothy Bush

A STEPPING STONE BOOK™

Random House 🏠 New York

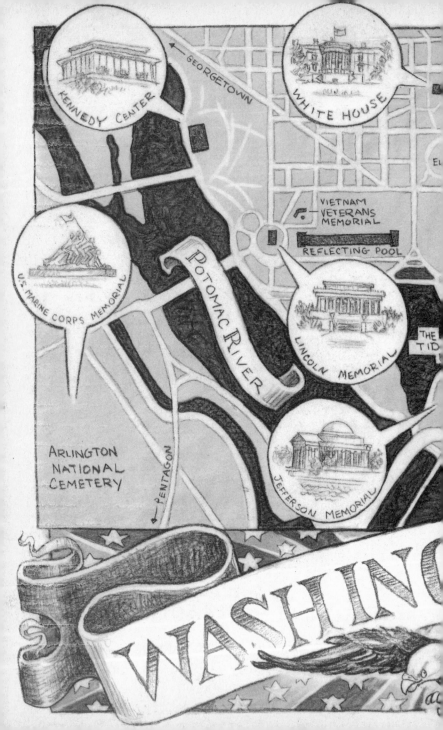

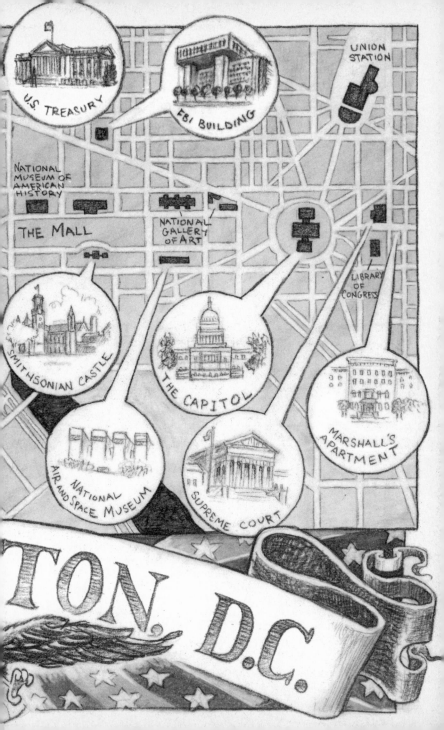

**To Judy and Ed, Jennifer and John,
little Jack and wee Will
—R.R.**

Photo credits: pp. 88–89 courtesy of the Library of Congress.

www.randomhouse.com/kids
www.steppingstonesbooks.com

Educators and librarians, for a variety of teaching tools, visit us at
www.randomhouse.com/teachers

Library of Congress Cataloging-in-Publication Data
Roy, Ron.
Trouble at the Treasury / by Ron Roy ; illustrated by Timothy Bush. — 1st ed.
     p.   cm. — (Capital mysteries ; #7)
"A Stepping Stone Book."
SUMMARY: KC and Marshall take a tour of the Bureau of Engraving and
Printing, and when they discover that someone has been stealing bricks
of newly printed money, they resolve to find the thief.
ISBN: 978-0-375-83969-6 (pbk.) — ISBN: 978-0-375-93969-3 (lib. bdg.)
[1. Money—Fiction. 2. Stealing—Fiction. 3. United States. Bureau of
Engraving and Printing—Fiction. 4. Washington (D.C.)—Fiction.
5. Mystery and detective stories.] I. Bush, Timothy, ill. II. Title.
III. Series: Roy, Ron. Capital mysteries ; #7.
PZ7.R8139Tr 2007 [Fic]—dc22 2006008558

Printed in the United States of America
10 9 8 7 6 5 4 3 2   First Edition

Contents

1. Money, Money Everywhere   1

2. No Stealing Allowed   11

3. A Very Expensive Brick   19

4. The Other President   32

5. The Man with the Flying Fingers   44

6. Three Suspects   55

7. Casey on the Case   65

8. Polly Talks   76

1

Money, Money Everywhere

"Hurry up, Marsh. It's almost two-thirty!" KC said.

"They can't start the tour without us," Marshall answered, racing after KC. "You're the president's stepdaughter!"

"Yeah, but I didn't tell them that," KC said.

It was the week before Christmas. KC Corcoran and her best friend, Marshall Li, had signed up for a tour of the Bureau of Engraving and Printing. The BEP is where paper money is printed in Washington, D.C.

KC had always wanted to see how

paper money was made. Marshall agreed to go on the tour with her, but she had to promise to visit the bug museum with him next week.

KC and Marshall ran up the steps of the massive BEP building and tugged open the heavy door.

Inside, a man in a blue uniform was talking with a small group of people. He held a clipboard and wore a name tag around his neck.

"Here they are," the man said to the group.

Four people turned and looked at KC and Marshall.

KC felt her face blush.

The man glanced at a list on his clipboard. "Are you Katherine Corcoran and Marshall Li?" he asked.

KC and Marshall nodded.

"Great, all seven are here," the man said. "I'm Vincent. Please hang your coats and bags over there on those hooks. We'll be going through metal detectors. So if you have any metal, leave it in your coat pockets."

"Can I take my camera with me?" KC asked.

"No pictures allowed, miss, sorry," Vincent said. "You can leave your camera with your coat."

They all walked to a row of brass hooks and left their coats. There were cubbies over the hooks for briefcases, hats, and gloves.

"Just like in school," KC whispered.

"Gee, I forgot to bring my lunch box," Marshall cracked.

"Don't worry about your personal belongings," Vincent said. "Jason will watch them." He pointed to a guard sitting behind a TV screen at a desk. Jason waved to the group.

"Are you ready to see millions of dollars being printed right before your eyes?" Vincent asked.

Everyone smiled and nodded.

"Do we get free samples?" one woman teased.

KC and Marshall laughed.

Vincent led the group through a metal detector. One man set off the alarm, so he had to remove his gold watch. He gave it to Jason, who put it in an envelope and slid it into his desk. "It'll be here when you come out, sir," he said.

After the metal detector, the group

went up a flight of stairs. At the top was a hallway with windows on both sides. The windows looked down on long rooms. "Those big pieces of green paper are sheets of money being printed," Vincent told the group.

Below one window, a huge machine was shooting sheets of green paper along a conveyor belt. Workers stood near the machine. They watched the paper carefully. "We have many machines that print the money," Vincent said. "Today, that one is printing hundred-dollar bills."

Vincent pointed to the conveyor belt. "Each of those sheets has thirty-two one-hundred-dollar bills," he said.

Everyone gawked as the sheets of money sped through the machine.

KC noticed that Marshall was having

fun. "Are you glad you came on the tour?" she asked.

Marshall nodded. "This is almost better than the insect room at the Smithsonian!" he said.

"Where do the sheets go after they're printed?" a woman asked.

"Look through the other set of windows," Vincent said.

Everyone turned around. The window looked over a room as long as a school bus. A single machine reached from end to end.

"That blade on the left is extremely sharp and heavy. It cuts the sheets into thirty-two single bills," Vincent told his group. "Notice that nobody touches the blade or the money. That blade would cut through a finger!"

"Yuck!" Marshall said.

The blade sliced easily through thick piles of money.

Vincent showed them a part of the machine that looked like a robot's arms and fingers. "The next section of the machine piles the bills into stacks. Each stack holds one thousand bills. Once the stacks are wrapped, they're called bricks."

KC did some quick math in her head. "So each brick is worth one hundred thousand dollars!" she said.

"That's right," Vincent said.

They all watched the money being cut, counted, stacked, and wrapped.

"Hey! That guy is touching the money!" Marshall said. "Is he counting it?"

At one part of the machine, far away from the blade, a man was taking handfuls of bills off the conveyor belt before they

8

were stacked and wrapped. He flipped through the bills, then put them back on the belt. He worked fast. His fingers flew over the money so quickly they were a blur.

"No, he's just checking some of the bills to make sure they are okay before they're wrapped into bricks," Vincent explained. "Bills that are bent or torn or have a printing error are destroyed."

A woman with long red hair entered the room. She wore a dark blue smock to protect her clothing. The woman was pushing a cart that held a large cardboard box half filled with trash. She stopped and emptied a small trash can into the box, then left the room.

"Where do the money bricks go?" a man asked.

Vincent pointed to the right end of the

machine. The conveyor belt ran through a small doorway and out of sight. "The bricks go through there to the vault," he said. "Eventually, the money will be sent to banks. Then it will find its way into stores and your wallets."

"No hundred-dollar bill ever finds its way to *my* wallet!" Marshall said.

Everyone laughed.

"How much money is made in a day?" a woman asked.

"Over six hundred million dollars," Vincent said with a straight face. "Every day."

2

No Stealing Allowed

Seven mouths dropped open.

"I know it seems unreal," Vincent continued, "but the machines print money around the clock. The only days they stop are Christmas and New Year's."

"Workers are here even at night?" KC asked.

Vincent nodded. "Yup. There are three shifts. Each shift lasts eight hours."

Just then a bell went off. "Three o'clock. This shift is over," Vincent said. Below them the workers left the room. Four more workers entered.

"Does anyone ever steal money?" KC asked.

Vincent laughed. "No. Every room has security cameras," he said. "They're never turned off. Our security staff checks the tapes several times a day. It would be impossible for anyone to take money without being seen by other workers or by the cameras."

The group stood and watched the bricks of money zip along the conveyor belt, then disappear through the small door.

"So where is the vault?" Marshall asked.

Vincent pointed at the floor. "Under the street," he said. "About twenty feet below where you're standing."

"H-how much money is down there?" Marshall whispered.

Vincent smiled. "I don't know for certain," he said. "But at least a few billion dollars. Well, that's the end of the tour, folks. I'll take you back to your coats and the exit."

"A few billion dollars right under our feet!" Marshall said. He and KC walked down the steps in front of the BEP. The sky had gotten darker and it looked like it would snow.

"Want to come back tonight and dig it up?" KC suggested with a sly smile.

"No way, it's too cold!" Marshall said. He pulled his coat up around his ears. "Can we get some hot chocolate? I'm freezing!"

"Why didn't you wear a hat?" KC said.

"I don't like hats," Marshall said. "They make my hair look dorky."

"Let's go in there." KC pointed across the street to a small restaurant. A sign in the window said THE VAULT. The door had been painted to look like the front of a giant safe. Fake money was stacked on a ledge inside the window.

They crossed the street and entered. People sat at tables and booths, eating and talking.

"Let's sit by the window," Marshall suggested.

"So you can touch that money?" KC asked.

Marshall grinned as he sat down. He ran his fingers over the stacks of money. "All fake," he moaned.

KC and Marshall took off their coats. A tall kid wearing an apron and a Santa hat came over holding a pad and pencil. "What can I get you?" he asked.

"Do you have hot chocolate?" KC asked.

"You bet. Whipped cream or marsh-mallows on top?" the waiter asked.

"Whipped cream, please!" KC said.

"I'll have the *Marsh*mallows," Marshall said, grinning at KC.

The waiter left, tucking his pad and pencil in a back pocket.

KC pulled her digital camera from her pack. "Hey, Marsh, let me take your picture next to all that money," she said.

Marshall leaned down so his face was almost buried in green bills.

He made a goofy face and KC snapped his picture. She checked the screen. "Good. Nice face, Marsh. This makes you look like you're a millionaire!" she said.

While they waited for their hot chocolates, KC glanced around the small room. At one table, a woman with red hair sat by herself. She wore dangly earrings made of little silver bells. In front of her was a mug with a tea-bag string hanging out of it and an open book.

The woman's lips were moving. It looked like she was repeating what she was reading. KC glanced at the book cover. It said LEARN ITALIAN FAST.

Every now and then, the woman shook her head, as if she'd gotten something wrong. When she moved her head, the bell earrings jingled.

"Marsh, that woman works in the BEP," KC whispered. "She emptied the trash during our tour."

"KC, you notice the weirdest things," Marshall said.

KC wanted to be a TV news anchor after college. And if there was one thing she was sure of, it was that news reporters paid attention!

The door opened with a blast of cold air. A tall man wearing a cowboy hat and a leather jacket walked in. He looked around, then headed for the table where the woman was studying Italian.

She looked up and beamed. She lowered the book as the man sat down. He gave her a quick kiss on the cheek.

KC leaned forward, hoping to hear what the man would say. But just then the waiter stepped in the way, blocking KC's view.

"Two hot chocolates!" he announced. He set the steaming drinks down. A candy cane stood in each mug.

KC stirred her chocolate with the candy cane. Marshall took a sip. "Youch, it's hot!" he gasped.

"It's *hot* chocolate, Marsh," KC said. "Duh!"

3

A Very Expensive Brick

The kids finished their hot chocolates, pulled on their coats, and left The Vault. They headed toward the Metro station to catch the train that would take them to the White House.

A cold wind was blowing right into their faces. KC shivered. Marshall's nose was red.

"Wait a sec," KC said. She pulled Marshall over to a pet-store window. Through the glass, they could see a box of puppies. They were all asleep in a pile. KC pulled out her digital camera and snapped a picture.

"Don't even think about it," Marshall

said. "You already have three cats and a dog in the White House."

"I just like to take pictures, Marsh," KC said. "Stand in front of the puppies and I'll get one of you, too." She stepped back and aimed her camera.

A man and woman stepped into the scene just as KC pushed the button.

"Oh, look, Travis, puppies!" the woman squealed.

She was bundled into a down ski jacket with a bright red scarf. Blond hair fell from under a red knit hat. The man wore a cowboy hat and leather jacket.

"No puppies," the man said. He gave the woman a kiss. "Come on, let's keep moving, honey."

The couple moved off with their arms around each other. KC snapped their picture as they walked away.

"Didn't we just see that man in the restaurant?" KC asked Marshall.

"So?" Marshall said. He tugged KC toward the Metro stop.

"So nothing," KC said. "But five minutes ago, he kissed that woman from the BEP. And now he's kissing a different lady."

"Don't be so nosy," Marshall said.

"I'm not being nosy," KC retorted. "I'm being observant!"

A half hour later, they were back home. Ever since KC's mom married the president, KC had lived in the White House. Arnold, a tall marine, stood guard outside the door of the president's private residence.

"How was your tour of the BEP?" he asked.

"It was totally awesome!" Marshall said. "Guess how much money they make in just one day!"

Arnold looked up at the ceiling and counted on his white-gloved fingers. "A million dollars?" he said.

"Try six hundred million!" Marshall said.

Arnold whistled as he opened the door. "Maybe I should ask the president for a raise," he whispered.

KC giggled. "I'll see what I can do," she whispered back.

She and Marshall hung their coats on a set of hooks in the kitchen.

The president's maid, Yvonne, was standing at the stove. "Did you have fun?" she asked.

"Guess how much money they make in a day," Marshall said, grinning.

"Six hundred million," Yvonne said.

"How did you know?" Marshall asked, surprised.

"I took my nephews on the tour last week," Yvonne said. "How about a snack?"

"That will be great," KC said. "Where are the president and my mom?"

Yvonne pointed to the closed door that led to the library. "Big doings in there," she said. "The Secretary of the Treasury is with them."

After a snack, KC and Marshall went upstairs to her room. "You want to play Monopoly?" she asked. "We can pretend it's real money."

They were still playing an hour later when they heard a knock on the bedroom door. The president and KC's mom walked in.

"Hi, how was the tour?" Lois asked.

"It was great," KC said. "We saw millions of dollars being printed!"

"And they keep it all in a vault right under the street!" Marshall added.

"Well, the vault is going to be short some money today," the president said. "Someone stole one hundred thousand dollars this morning."

KC and Marshall stared at President Thornton.

"What do you mean?" KC asked.

"They stack one thousand bills together into a package they call a brick," the president said. "A brick of hundred-dollar bills is missing."

"We saw those bricks on our tour!" KC said.

"Actually, the same amount went missing last week. The Bureau thought that one was just a counting mistake," the

president went on. "Now they're sure that someone stole the money."

"But the tour guide told us it was impossible to steal money," Marshall said. "Because of the security cameras!"

"I know," the president said. "Impossible or not, someone did it . . . twice." He smiled at his stepdaughter and Marshall. "You kids didn't happen to notice anyone stuffing money in a pocket, did you?"

"No, we were too busy watching the machines making it," Marshall said.

"Well, nothing we can do about it," Lois said. "Kids, Zachary and I are going out of town tomorrow, so we're eating early tonight. Five minutes, okay?"

"Okay, but can Marshall roll first?" KC asked. "He's going to land on my hotel and I'll be rich!"

"Fine, but then come right down to

eat," Lois said. She and the president left the room.

Marshall picked up the dice and rolled.

KC crossed her fingers.

He landed on KC's hotel. "Rats, this game is rigged!"

KC grinned. As she counted the money Marshall handed her, she had an idea. "Marsh, remember the guy who was checking the money? You asked Vincent about him."

"Yeah, the guy with the fast fingers," Marshall said. His eyes opened wide. "Are you thinking what I'm thinking?"

KC nodded. "Maybe he didn't put all the money back on the conveyor belt after he checked it! Maybe some of it went somewhere else, like inside his shirt!"

"But what about all the cameras?" Marshall asked. "Someone would have noticed if the guy took any bills. They watch the tapes every day."

"I guess so," KC said. In her mind, she was seeing the man handling the money. She had not noticed him stick any bills in his pocket. All she saw was those fingers flying back and forth. "Come on, let's go eat."

Yvonne set platters of fried chicken, mashed potatoes, and thin green beans on the table.

"Thanks, Yvonne, this all looks and smells delicious," the president said.

"You're welcome, sir," Yvonne said. "Will you need me anymore? This is my bowling night."

"Go and have fun," Lois said. "We'll take care of the dishes."

Just then the phone rang.

"I'd better get that," the president said.

"The folks at the BEP are checking the camera videotapes. Maybe they've already caught our crook!"

The president left the table, but came back in less than three minutes.

"No luck," he said. He sat down and picked up his napkin. "The tape for today had nothing unusual. It certainly didn't show some worker hiding a hundred thousand dollars in his lunch box!"

"Do they ever search the people who work there?" KC asked.

"I don't know for sure," the president said. "But I'll look into it."

"What about the serial numbers on the bills?" Marshall asked. "If the crook tries to spend the money, can't they catch him that way?"

The president nodded. "Yes, Marsh," he said. "Those numbers are already being sent to stores and banks. But if I were the thief, I wouldn't spend the money right away. I'd hide it for a year or two, and wait."

"Well, if I had stolen the money, I'd sneak it into some foreign country," Lois added, "where it would be very hard to track."

KC looked up. Something her parents had just said made a thought pop into her head. But the idea was gone a second later.

KC's mom and the president started talking about their trip tomorrow.

KC leaned over and whispered in Marshall's ear.

"Let's go back to the BEP tomorrow," she said.

"Why?" Marshall asked.

"I want to watch that videotape," KC

30

said. "Maybe we can get them to pause the tape. We might see that guy stashing some of the money in his clothes."

Marshall snorted. "KC, they'll never let two kids look at that videotape," he said. "Especially now that they've had another robbery!"

"They'd let the president see it," KC whispered.

"He's going out of town, remember?" Marshall said.

KC grinned at Marshall. "I know that," she said, keeping her voice low. "I was thinking of the *other* president!"

4

The Other President

Marshall stared at her with a blank look on his face. "The other president . . . oh, you mean Casey Marshall!"

"Yes!" KC said.

When KC and Marshall first met President Thornton, some evil scientists had locked him in the White House basement and cloned him. KC and Marshall figured out the plot, and the scientists went to prison.

But the clone was a nice guy. The president gave him a small apartment in the White House. "Who knows when I might need a body double," the president had explained.

KC and Marshall took the elevator to the lower level of the White House. "Casey likes to watch movies down here," KC said.

But the presidential movie theater was dark.

"Shh, I hear something," Marshall said.

"It's water," KC said. "He must be in the swimming pool!"

They found Casey Marshall swimming laps in the long blue pool. The kids waited till he came up for air, and KC handed him a towel.

"Well, hello," Casey said. "What brings you down here?"

Casey climbed out of the pool. He looked identical to KC's stepfather, from his brown eyes to his dark hair. Of course, usually the president didn't wear a wet bathing suit.

"How'd you like to go somewhere fun with us tomorrow?" KC asked.

"Where?" Casey asked. He rubbed his hair with the towel.

"To the Bureau of Engraving and Printing," KC said.

"Why?" he asked. "You two look like you're up to something."

KC and Marshall told Casey about the two thefts. "We think the thief is someone we saw yesterday on our tour," KC explained. "But we need to watch the videotapes from the hidden cameras to be sure."

"I told KC they probably wouldn't let us," Marshall went on.

"So we want you to come with us and pretend to be the president," KC said. "They'd have to let you see the tapes!"

Casey wrapped the towel around his

neck. "I can't lie and say I'm the president," he said.

"You won't have to lie," KC assured the clone. She told him the rest of the plan as they went to his apartment. It was near the White House bowling alley.

Casey opened his closet. "What should I wear?" he asked.

"Something my stepdad would wear," KC said.

Casey pulled a dark blue suit off a hanger. "How about this?"

"That's perfect," KC said. "The president has three others just like it."

Casey grinned. "I know. He gave me this one."

They picked out a white shirt, red tie, and black shoes.

"Okay, Mom and the president are leaving right after breakfast tomorrow,"

KC told Casey. "Can you meet me and Marshall in the kitchen at nine-thirty? They should be gone by then."

"I sure hope I don't get in trouble for this," Casey said.

"You won't," KC said. "In fact, the president will be happy when we tell him you helped us catch the crook!"

The next morning, Marshall got up early and biked to the White House. He was in time for breakfast, as usual. Yvonne made scrambled eggs and cut up fresh fruit. The president was sitting at the table, wearing a dark blue suit with a red tie. KC caught Marshall's eye and started to giggle.

"What's funny, honey?" the president asked.

"It's a secret," KC said. She was thinking of Casey downstairs wearing an identical suit.

"Well, we have to go," the president said, standing up. "What are your plans for the day, kids?"

"That's a secret, too," KC said.

"Boy, I live in a house filled with secrets!" the president said. He gave them a wave and thanked Yvonne as he walked out the door.

Three minutes later, the kitchen door opened again and Casey walked in.

Yvonne stared. "Sir?" she said. "Did you forget something?"

"I don't think so," Casey said. "May I please have some scrambled eggs?"

"But, Mr. President, you just ate," Yvonne said. "And when I offered you seconds, you told me you were full."

KC and Marshall burst out laughing.

"Yvonne, this is Casey Marshall, not the president. He's going out with us to do something for the president."

"Oh, I feel so foolish," Yvonne said. "I don't usually see you in a suit, Casey. Let me fix you a plate."

After Casey ate breakfast, he, KC, and Marshall all put on coats and left.

KC had called a taxi. It was waiting right outside. The driver jumped out and opened the rear door with a huge grin on his face. "Good morning, Mr. President!" he chirped.

"Good morning," Casey said. He stepped into the taxi. KC and Marshall squeezed in after him.

Ten minutes later, the kids and Casey entered through the BEP's front door. A young man in a blue blazer approached them. A name tag hung from a chain around his neck. It said that he was an aide and his name was Peter. Peter opened his mouth; then closed it again when he noticed Casey.

"Good m-morning, M-Mr. P-President," Peter finally stammered.

"Good morning, young man," Casey said.

"The president has heard about the money that was stolen," KC said. "We'd like to see yesterday's videotapes, please."

Peter was still staring at Casey. "Um, I need to . . . um, just a minute, please." He hurried away.

"Did I fool him?" Casey whispered.

"Totally," Marshall said. "His face was as red as your necktie!"

The kid came back with a gray-haired man in a dark suit. "Mr. President, how may we help, sir?" he asked.

"I'd like to see yesterday's videotapes, please," Casey said.

"Ah, yes," the man said. "Follow me, please."

He led them to an elevator. Inside, he pushed a button and KC felt the elevator car going up. When it stopped, they stepped out and walked to a black door. A sign on the door said

PRIVATE
DO NOT ENTER

The door was opened by a woman wearing thick glasses. When she noticed Casey, she said, "Oh my goodness!" and backed away.

They entered a large square room. The lighting was dim, and the space was half dark. Nearly every inch of wall held a screen. Some of them were blank, but others showed flickering images.

A tall man walked over to the group. "I'm Travis Royce, floor manager. Can I help here?" he asked. Then his eyes fell on Casey. "Mr. President! Good morning, sir!"

Casey nodded at the man. "I'd like to see yesterday's videotapes," he said again.

"Oh, you're here about the robbery," Mr. Royce said. "We use compact discs now, sir. I've reviewed them several times myself, and I showed them to my boss. They're still on my desk."

As Casey followed Mr. Royce, KC grabbed Marshall's arm.

"Recognize him?" she whispered.

"No, should I?" Marshall asked.

"The restaurant yesterday," KC hissed. "He came in and sat with that woman with red hair. The one who works in the room where they cut the money. Then a few minutes later, we saw him near the pet store all lovey-dovey with that blonde!"

5

The Man with the Flying Fingers

Mr. Royce had stopped at one corner of the room. A computer was open on the desk. A group of TV screens hung on the wall. Two of the screens showed people working around the money-printing machines.

Travis Royce waved at the screens. "What you're seeing is happening right now, downstairs," he said.

KC studied the two screens. It was like watching a movie of what she and Marshall had seen yesterday. At the bottom of each screen was the time and date.

Mr. Royce picked up three discs from his desk. Each one had "December 19" written on the plastic sleeve. "These are from yesterday's three shifts, sir," he said to Casey Marshall. "Would you like to see them all?"

"Do you know when the money was taken?" KC asked.

"It went missing during the first shift," he said. He chose one of the three CDs. "That runs from seven in the morning till three in the afternoon."

Marshall groaned. "Watching the whole shift would take eight hours!" he said.

"We've been able to narrow it down," Mr. Royce said. "We count the bricks several times during each shift. The staff thinks the missing brick of bills was lifted between eleven and twelve, just before lunch."

He tapped a few keys on the computer.

Suddenly they were looking at the sheets of money being cut, then speeding along the conveyor belt in small piles. "This is yesterday morning at eleven," Mr. Royce said.

KC noticed that the woman with red hair was there. She was wiping parts of the machinery with a large cleaning cloth. The time at the bottom showed that it was eleven o'clock, Wednesday, December 19.

"Excuse me, who is that woman?" KC asked.

"That's Polly Fine," Mr. Royce said. "She's a good worker. She keeps the rooms clean on her shift."

"What about him?" KC asked. She pointed to the man who was grabbing money, checking it for problems, then placing the bills back on the conveyor belt.

"That's Eddie Yump," Mr. Royce said. "We call him 'Fast Eddie' because his fingers move so quickly. He's been here for about five years."

They all watched as Eddie snatched, flipped, and replaced money over and over again. His hands were a blur.

"Can you stop the picture?" KC asked Mr. Royce.

"Sure." Mr. Royce pressed a key, and the image on the computer screen froze. Eddie Yump held a fistful of bills close to his eyes. Polly Fine was in the background. One hand was raised to wipe something with her cleaning cloth. Two other workers in the room were also frozen, as if they'd been playing a game of statues.

"Can you make it bigger?" KC asked. She leaned forward.

Mr. Royce clicked the mouse. The picture grew larger.

"Can you make it move again, but real slow?" KC asked.

Now Polly was wiping in slow motion. Her little reindeer earrings waved back and forth as she moved. Eddie Yump riffled the bills in his hand. This time it was slow enough for KC to see each bill.

"Does anyone else touch the money?" KC asked.

"Once the sheets are cut into bills, only Eddie handles them," Mr. Royce said. He speeded up the disc and they all watched Eddie Yump doing his job.

"Excuse me, but if you think Eddie is the thief, you're wrong," Mr. Royce said. "Trust me, he's the most honest person I know. Before I hired him, I got an excellent report from his last boss."

"Where did he work before he came here?" Marshall asked.

"He was a card dealer in a casino," Mr. Royce said.

KC stared at the man on the screen as he replaced the money on the belt, and took more. "No wonder his hands are so fast!" she said.

"Can we see the vault?" Marshall asked.

Mr. Royce shook his head. "No, I'm afraid not. It's off-limits to the public."

"Why, I'd love to see that myself!" Casey said.

"Oh, of course, Mr. President," Mr. Royce said. "I'll get the shift manager to take you down there."

He picked up a telephone, spoke into it softly, then hung up. "Ms. Slye will be here in a second."

While Casey and Mr. Royce shook hands, KC turned to Marshall.

"Why did you ask to see the vault?" she asked.

"Are you kidding? This is my only chance to see a kajillion dollars up close!" Marshall said. "It'll be even better than the tour!"

The elevator door opened and a tall woman came over to them. She held her hand out to Casey.

"Mr. President, welcome to the BEP. I'm Gladys Slye. I understand you want to see the cookie jar," she said.

Casey gave her a blank look. "Cookie jar?"

"Oh, that's what I call the vault," Ms. Slye explained. "Won't you join me?"

She stepped back into the elevator and the others followed.

"The vault is beneath the street and under this building," Ms. Slye said as the elevator went down.

At the bottom, they stepped into a wide hallway. The walls, floor, and ceiling were all built of steel. As they followed Ms. Slye, their footsteps echoed around them.

Ms. Slye stopped at a closed metal door. She tapped a code into a keypad on the wall, and the door opened. They all stepped through. Right away they saw two guards standing in front of a second door. This door was thick and broad, like on a castle.

Ms. Slye nodded at the guards. Then she pressed her eye up against a sort of window in the wall next to the door. A small light near the window turned green.

"That scans my eyes for a match," she explained. "We used to use fingerprints, but they can be faked."

They all heard a click, and the vault door slowly opened.

"After you, sir," Ms. Slye said.

Casey entered the vault. KC and Marshall followed him into the gigantic space. The room was as large as KC and Marshall's whole school! Each wall was lined with metal shelves, from the floor to the ceiling. Every shelf held piles and piles of money bricks.

KC found that she couldn't speak. Even Marshall was silent. His eyes looked as big as golf balls.

Ms. Slye picked up a stack and stroked the money the way KC petted her cats. "I know it's astonishing," she said. "I come in here several times a day, and I never get used to it."

"How much money is there?" Casey asked.

Ms. Slye returned the money to the shelf. Then she tapped a few keys on a laptop computer. "Right now, the total is nine billion, seven hundred and thirty million, six hundred thousand, five hundred dollars," she said.

6
Three Suspects

KC, Marshall, and Casey just stared at Ms. Slye.

"How do you know?" KC managed to ask.

"Our computers count it for us," Ms. Slye said. "Each day, the newly printed bills get counted several times. Then they are added to what's already here in the vault."

"Does your computer ever make mistakes?" Casey asked. "I was told about the missing money. . . ."

Ms. Slye looked at Casey. "Mr. President, we don't know how to explain what happened to that money," she said. "But the Treasury Department has its own detectives, and they were on the case minutes after the theft was discovered."

"When was the other money taken?" Marshall asked. "You know, the other brick."

"That was last week," Ms. Slye said.

"Which day and shift?" KC asked. She was glad that Marshall had thought to ask his question.

"I believe the money was taken at the same time on the same day last week," Ms. Slye said. "That would have been between eleven in the morning and noon on Wednesday, December 12th."

KC thought about that for a moment. "Can anybody besides you get into this vault?" she asked the woman.

"During the shift when the money disappeared, I am the only one who has access to this vault," she answered. "Of course, there are different managers for the other shifts, but no money was reported missing on those shifts." Her voice sounded tight.

"So you were the manager when the money was stolen, on both Wednesdays?" KC asked.

Ms. Slye nodded. "Yes" was all she said.

Just then they all heard a quiet chirping noise. Ms. Slye pulled a cell phone from her pocket. She flipped it open, glanced at the screen, and snapped it shut again. "I'm needed upstairs," she said. "May I take you to the exit?"

"That will be fine," Casey said. "And thank you for your time."

"The pleasure was mine, Mr. President," Ms. Slye said.

KC didn't think Ms. Slye looked

pleased at all. Her face had turned red, and she looked embarrassed or angry. Or both.

They stepped out of the vault. The ten-inch-thick steel door made only a soft swooshing noise as Ms. Slye swung it shut.

Back at the White House, KC had a lot to think about. She flopped down in a chair. Her cats, Lost and Found, came running. The president's cat, George, was cleaning his paws by the fireplace. Natasha, the White House dog, was sleeping on the floor.

"Well, now we know two people who had a chance to steal that money," KC said. " 'Fast' Eddie Yump and Ms. Slye."

Marshall shook his head. "The manager?" he blurted out. "No way."

"Marsh, she told us she's the only one who can enter the vault on her shift," KC said. "And she was working both times the money was stolen. She could've grabbed a brick from the vault and hidden it in her purse or something."

"But they count the money," Marshall said. "She'd get caught."

KC stood up and paced around the room. "Remember that laptop in the vault?" she asked. "What if Ms. Slye changed the total? Then no one would know any money was missing. Everyone would think the money got stolen before it ever reached the vault."

"Or it could have been Eddie Yump," Marshall said. "He gets my vote. Don't forget, he used to work in a casino. He's probably a card cheat!"

KC sat down again. "We have two suspects. But we can't prove either one of them took the money," she said.

Yvonne came in carrying a grocery bag. "Hi, gang," she said.

KC and Marshall helped her put the groceries away. Yvonne was in a good mood. She was singing Christmas carols, "Let It Snow" and then "Silver Bells."

Suddenly KC almost dropped the carton of milk she was holding.

"What?" Marshall asked, looking at his friend.

"That song about the bells. It reminds me of something, but I don't know what," KC said. "Something important. Keep singing, Yvonne."

Yvonne sang the entire song.

KC paced around the kitchen again, dodging the kittens and Yvonne.

"I'll have lunch ready in about twenty minutes," Yvonne said at the song's end. "How about some sandwiches? And I just bought marshmallows for hot chocolate."

KC stopped pacing. She stared at Yvonne.

"You don't want any hot chocolate?" Yvonne asked.

"That's it!" KC shouted. "Yvonne, you're a genius!"

"I am? Well, thank you!" Yvonne said.

"Can someone tell me what's going on?" Marshall said.

"Marsh, yesterday when we had hot chocolate in that restaurant after the tour, we saw that redheaded woman, right?" KC asked. "Mr. Royce said her name was Polly."

"Yep. She was reading a book about learning Italian," Marshall said.

"And she was wearing tiny bells for earrings," KC went on. "I heard them tinkle when she moved her head."

Marshall just stared at KC. "And this is exciting because?" he said.

"Because she wasn't wearing them on that disc we saw this morning!" KC announced. "Remember I asked Mr. Royce to make the picture bigger? Well, I really wanted to see Fast Eddie up close. But at the same time I noticed that Polly was wearing reindeer earrings."

Marshall shook his head. "I don't get it," he said.

"The part of the disc we looked at was taken at eleven o'clock yesterday morning," KC explained. "And Polly was wearing reindeer earrings. But when we saw her in the restaurant at three o'clock, she had on little bell earrings."

"Maybe she changed her earrings sometime between eleven o'clock and three o'clock," Marshall suggested.

"I have another idea," KC said. "Maybe the disc we looked at wasn't from yesterday."

"But, KC, the date was right on the disc," Marshall said. "It said eleven a.m., Wednesday, December 19th, which was yesterday. I saw it!"

KC nodded. "I saw it, too," she said. "I just don't believe it."

7
Casey on the Case

Yvonne served the sandwiches and mugs of hot chocolate. KC talked while Marshall gobbled his food.

"This is what I think happened," KC said. "Somehow, Polly stole the money yesterday morning without the other workers there seeing her. But she knew the security cameras would catch her, and the theft would be on that disc. So she went up to Mr. Royce's office and got rid of yesterday's disc. She switched it with a disc recorded on another day."

"A day when she was wearing different earrings," Marshall said. "Now I get it. But I don't believe it!"

KC glared at him. "You don't? Why?"

"For one thing, how would she get into Mr. Royce's office?" Marshall asked. "She'd need keys. And she'd have to switch the discs when the office was empty. Which is never."

"Okay, she's a cleaning lady, right? So maybe she has her own keys. Maybe she went up there between shifts or something," KC said. "I don't know how, but I'm sure Polly did it!"

"And did she also change the time and date on that disc we looked at?" Marshall asked.

KC took a sip of her drink. "Plenty of people know computer stuff," she said. "Maybe she took computer classes in high school or college."

"Or . . . ," Marshall said, "maybe Polly and Mr. Royce are in it together!" He took a sip of his hot chocolate. It left a marsh-mallow mustache on his upper lip.

KC nodded slowly. "Marsh, you may be right!" she said. "Let's go—we're having a talk with Polly Fine!"

Marshall looked at KC over the top of his mug. "We are? When?"

"Today at three o'clock, when Polly gets off her shift," KC said. She glanced at the stove clock. It was already two o'clock.

Marshall grinned. "Are we going to arrest her and lock her in the Oval Office till the president gets back?" he asked.

"Marsh, that's an even better idea than your last one!" KC said.

"Uh-oh, I should've kept my mouth shut," Marshall muttered.

At three o'clock, KC and Marshall walked into the restaurant called The

Vault. "There she is!" KC whispered.

Polly Fine was sitting alone again. She was reading her Italian book and sipping tea.

KC and Marshall walked over to her table.

"Excuse me," KC said. "Are you Polly Fine?"

The woman looked up. She had pretty green eyes and a nice smile.

"Yes, I'm Polly," she said. "Do I know you?"

KC scooted into a chair without being invited. "My stepfather is President Thornton," she said. She kept her voice low. "And he'd like to meet you. He's right outside in a taxi."

Polly Fine blinked several times. "The president wants to meet me?" she said. "You're kidding, right?"

Marshall walked outside and said something through the taxi window. Someone who looked like the president stepped out of the taxi. Of course, it was really Casey Marshall in his blue suit and red tie. He smiled and waved at Polly through the restaurant window.

"Why does the president want to talk to *me*?" Polly asked.

"He needs your help on something that's top-secret," KC said. "I can't tell you any more with all these people listening. But it's very important! You have to come to the White House right now!"

"Well, okay," Polly said. She left some money on the table, slipped into her coat, and followed KC out of The Vault.

Marshall sat up front with the taxi driver, and KC sat between Polly and Casey in the back.

Casey held his hand out. "Miss Fine, I'm delighted to meet you. Thank you for agreeing to come to the White House."

"Mr. President, I am thrilled!" Polly gushed. "How can I help you?"

Casey put a finger to his lips. He nodded toward the driver in the front seat. "Later," he whispered.

The cab dropped them off at the rear of the White House. KC and Marshall took Polly to the president's private library.

Before going downstairs, Casey pulled KC and Marshall aside. "Thank you for introducing me to Polly," he said. "She's the prettiest woman I've ever met!"

When they were seated in the library, KC felt as if her stomach were filled with butterflies. Polly seemed even more nervous.

Polly looked around the room. It was decorated with books, fresh flowers, and portraits of former presidents. "Why am I here?" she asked.

"We know about the money," KC said. "We saw the discs in Mr. Royce's office."

KC crossed her fingers. She prayed that she'd gotten this right. What would they do if Polly suddenly jumped up and ran screaming from the room? Or if she turned on them? KC didn't think Polly looked like a dangerous criminal, but you never knew.

But Polly didn't jump or scream. She just stared at KC. Her pretty eyes filled with tears. She began to sob.

KC handed her a box of tissues.

Just then the president walked through the door. He was still wearing his blue suit and red tie. "Oh, excuse me," he said.

KC jumped up and left the room, pulling on her stepfather's hand.

"What's going on?" he asked KC. "I just passed Casey. He smiled like he knew a big secret, but he didn't say a word. Who's that woman?"

"That's part of the secret," KC told her stepfather.

"Another one?" the president said. "When do I get to hear about all these secrets?"

"Right now, if you'll come and sit with us," KC said. "Let me do the talking, and you'll learn how the money was stolen from the BEP!"

The president walked into the room, nodded at Marshall, and sat.

"The president would like to hear your story now, Polly," KC said.

Polly shook her head. "I can't. I'm too

73

embarrassed," she mumbled into her handful of tissues.

"Please don't be embarrassed," the president said in a kind voice. "Tell us your story, Polly."

"I didn't mean to do it," Polly finally said. "I never stole anything before this, ever! About six months ago, a man walked into the shop where I was working. I was doing magic tricks for a few children."

"You're a magician?" KC asked.

Polly nodded, drying her tears. "I trained myself while I sold magic supplies. Anyway, the man watched me doing my tricks. When the children left, he came over and began talking to me. Then he offered me a job. He promised me more money than I was making in the shop."

"The job was at the BEP, right?" Marshall asked.

Polly nodded.

"And was the man's name Travis Royce?" KC asked.

"Yes," Polly said. "We're going to be married."

8
Polly Talks

KC thought about the blond woman she'd seen Travis Royce kissing by the pet shop. She got up and took her digital camera off a shelf.

"We began dating the week after I started working at the Bureau," Polly continued. "A month ago, he asked me to marry him. He said his dream was to live in Italy and open a small restaurant. He said he didn't have enough money, and could I help him. I said yes, I'd do anything!"

Polly looked up. "That's when he told me his plan to steal money from the cutting room in the BEP," she said. "At first I said no. I wouldn't steal. But Travis said we couldn't go to Italy without at least a half million dollars. He said we couldn't get married, either. So I . . . I agreed to take one brick each week for five weeks."

"A half million dollars," the president said. "And with your skill as a magician, you were able to lift the money without being noticed."

Polly nodded. "Yes, sir. When I was cleaning, it was easy to snatch a brick off the conveyor belt. But I knew the cameras would see everything. Travis told me not to worry. He had that part all planned. He worked in security, watching the screens upstairs. He said he'd edit the tapes, or get rid of them or something. He promised no one would ever see what the cameras saw."

KC turned on her digital camera,

clicked to one of the photos, and handed the camera to Polly.

Polly looked at the picture of Travis Royce and the blond woman kissing near the pet shop.

KC expected Polly to begin crying again. But the woman surprised KC. She smiled sadly and shook her head.

"Oh no," she whispered. "I saw them together one day. He said she was just his cousin. I've been such a fool." She handed the camera back to KC.

No one in the room knew what to say.

Finally, Polly broke the silence. "The money is in a safety-deposit box at my bank," she said. "Travis and I each have a key. I can get the money for you now, if you want."

"Thank you," the president said. "But what shall we do about Mr. Travis Royce?"

Polly sniffed, gulped, then seemed to make a difficult decision.

"Would it help if I called Travis and got him to meet me at my bank?" she asked. "I could tell him some story . . . like the money is gone from the box or something."

"That would be excellent," the president said. "And I'll make sure Mr. Royce has a welcoming committee to meet him there!"

KC, Marshall, and the president sat in the rear of a long black car with tinted windows. Casey Marshall sat up front, next to the driver. They were parked in front of the First National Bank, not far from the Bureau of Engraving and Printing.

Polly Fine was standing in front of the

bank. A few yards away, two men were changing a car tire. Across the street, a woman stood behind a pretzel cart, blowing on her fingers to keep them warm. She had two customers.

"There he is!" KC said.

Travis Royce came jogging along the sidewalk. He stopped in front of Polly and began yelling and waving his arms in the air. Travis grabbed Polly's arm and started to march her toward the bank.

They didn't get far. The two tire changers and the pretzel seller moved in. "FBI! Freeze!" one of the men said. The other officers surrounded Travis Royce. The pretzel seller flicked open a pair of handcuffs. She snapped them around Travis's wrists.

Polly stood there watching, her face white. The FBI agents put Travis into

their car. When it drove away, KC and Marshall ran over to Polly.

"Polly, are you okay?" KC asked.

"Were you scared?" Marshall asked.

Polly let out a long breath. "Yes, I was shaking in my boots," she said.

Then she squared her shoulders. "Come on," she said. "Let's go get the money."

Polly, the president, KC, and Marshall all trooped into the bank. Polly pulled a little key out of her bag. She showed it to a woman working at a desk. Behind her, a thick metal door stood open.

"Can I help you?" the woman asked Polly.

"Yes, I need to get into my safety-deposit box," Polly answered.

"Certainly," the woman said. She slid a paper in front of Polly. "Please sign this."

Polly signed the paper. "Come in with me," she whispered to KC and Marshall.

The woman led them through the open door into a narrow room. She stopped in front of a wall divided into hundreds of boxes. Each box front had two keyholes. The woman and Polly each inserted a key. The box door opened, and the woman pulled Polly's box out.

"Just lock it up when you're done," the woman said. She went back to her desk.

Polly lifted the lid off the box. Inside were nestled two money bricks.

"Wow," Marshall said. "Can I touch them?"

Polly nodded.

Marshall ran his fingers over the two bricks. He grinned. "It feels better than Monopoly money!" he said.

Polly wrapped the money bricks in her

scarf. Outside the room, she handed the package to the president. He pulled out his cell phone and called the BEP. "Someone will come right over and get the money," he told Polly.

They all got back into the long black car. "Well, you three certainly had an exciting day!" the president said to Casey, KC, and Marshall.

"Don't blame me and Casey!" Marshall said. "KC made us do it!"

Everyone laughed.

"I hope you don't mind too much that I pretended to be you," Casey said to the president.

"Not at all," the president said.

KC looked at Polly, then took her hand. "What's going to happen to Polly?" KC asked.

"First, we'll drop her off at her home,"

the president said. "Polly, my lawyers will help you. You stole money, but you gave it back. You also led us right to the real criminal, Mr. Travis Royce."

The president asked the driver to take Polly to her apartment building. "My lawyers will call you tomorrow," he told her.

"Thank you, sir," Polly said, "for everything." She got out of the car and walked into her building. Casey stared after Polly as she walked away. When the door shut behind her, he sighed and turned back to KC, Marshall, and the president.

Casey blushed. "Mr. President, I was wondering if you knew where I could take foreign-language lessons."

"What language are you interested in learning?" the president asked.

"Italian," Casey said.

KC and Marshall started to laugh.

"What's so funny?" President Thornton asked.

"It's a secret," KC said, and she and Marshall kept right on laughing.

**Don't miss KC and Marshall's
next exciting adventure!**

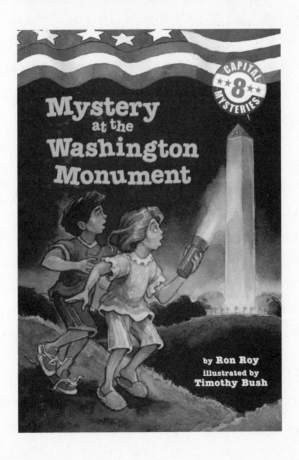

Did you know?

When they read the word *treasure,* most people think of money. In the late 1700s, the U.S. Department of the Treasury was created. One of the Treasury's duties was to make money and send it to banks.

The Treasury Building is located in Washington, D.C., right next door to the White House. You can find a picture of the Treasury Building on the back of a ten-dollar bill. But that building is not where our money is made. In 1792, the U.S. Mint was created to make coins.

Our paper money is printed at the Bureau of Engraving and Printing—BEP for short. The BEP has two locations, one in Fort Worth, Texas, and the other in Washington,

D.C. They make around $635 million in bills every day!

When new money is made, it's sent to the Treasury Building. From there, the money is shipped to banks all over the United States.

Some fun "MONEY" facts:

$ "Paper" money is made of linen and cotton, not paper.
$ The BEP uses about 18 tons of ink a day to make money.
$ To stack dollar bills one mile high, you would need more than 14 million bills!

A to Z Mysteries®

Help Dink, Josh, and Ruth Rose . . .